The Homestead Kids Book Series

Welcome Home

Rosie's Treasure

Michelle's Mission

Adee's Red Blanket

Coloring Book for Books 1-4

Coloring Book
for Books 1-4

By Brian Combs

The Homestead Kids Book Series

www.thehomesteadkidsbooks.com

Copyright 2023 © ETX Homeschool Publishing, LLC

All rights reserved. No part of this book may be reproduced or used in any manner whatsoever without the express written permission of the publisher except for the use of brief quotations in a book review.

By Brian Combs
Illustrations by Viviana Moyano.

The Homestead Kids Book Series   www.thehomesteadkidsbooks.com

Illustrations by Viviana Moyana

The Homestead Kids Book Series   www.thehomesteadkidsbooks.com

Illustrations by Viviana Moyana

The Homestead Kids Book Series	www.thehomesteadkidsbooks.com

Illustrations by Viviana Moyana

The Homestead Kids Book Series www.thehomesteadkidsbooks.com

Illustrations by Viviana Moyana

The Homestead Kids Book Series www.thehomesteadkidsbooks.com

Illustrations by Viviana Moyana

The Homestead Kids Book Series   www.thehomesteadkidsbooks.com

Illustrations by Viviana Moyana

The Homestead Kids Book Series www.thehomesteadkidsbooks.com

Illustrations by Viviana Moyana

The Homestead Kids Book Series　　　　　　　www.thehomesteadkidsbooks.com

Illustrations by Viviana Moyana

The Homestead Kids Book Series www.thehomesteadkidsbooks.com

Illustrations by Viviana Moyana

The Homestead Kids Book Series   www.thehomesteadkidsbooks.com

Illustrations by Viviana Moyana

The Homestead Kids Book Series www.thehomesteadkidsbooks.com

Illustrations by Viviana Moyana

The Homestead Kids Book Series · www.thehomesteadkidsbooks.com

Illustrations by Viviana Moyana

The Homestead Kids Book Series		www.thehomesteadkidsbooks.com

Illustrations by Viviana Moyana

The Homestead Kids Book Series　　　　　www.thehomesteadkidsbooks.com

Illustrations by Viviana Moyana

The Homestead Kids Book Series	www.thehomesteadkidsbooks.com

Illustrations by Viviana Moyana

The Homestead Kids Book Series www.thehomesteadkidsbooks.com

Illustrations by Viviana Moyana

The Homestead Kids Book Series   www.thehomesteadkidsbooks.com

Illustrations by Viviana Moyana

The Homestead Kids Book Series	www.thehomesteadkidsbooks.com

Illustrations by Viviana Moyana

The Homestead Kids Book Series   www.thehomesteadkidsbooks.com

Illustrations by Viviana Moyana

The Homestead Kids Book Series — www.thehomesteadkidsbooks.com

Illustrations by Viviana Moyana

The Homestead Kids Book Series　　　　　www.thehomesteadkidsbooks.com

Illustrations by Viviana Moyana

The Homestead Kids Book Series   www.thehomesteadkidsbooks.com

Illustrations by Viviana Moyana

The Homestead Kids Book Series   www.thehomesteadkidsbooks.com

Illustrations by Viviana Moyana

The Homestead Kids Book Series	www.thehomesteadkidsbooks.com

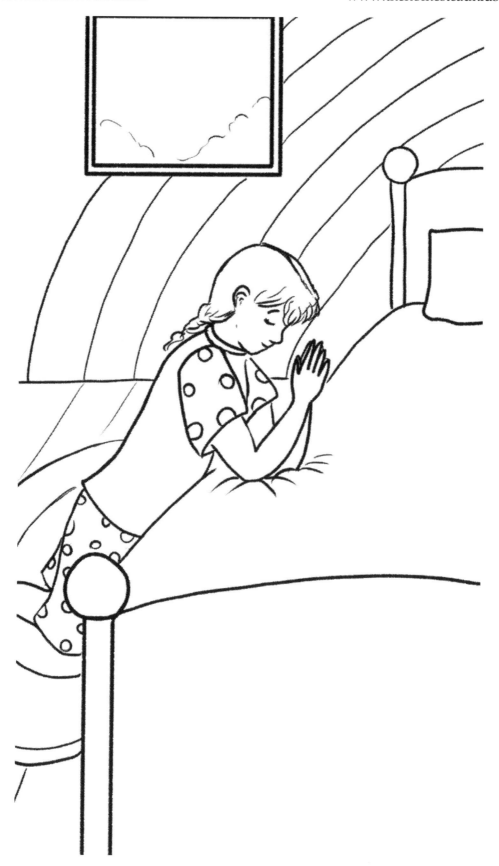

Illustrations by Viviana Moyana

The Homestead Kids Book Series www.thehomesteadkidsbooks.com

Illustrations by Viviana Moyana

The Homestead Kids Book Series   www.thehomesteadkidsbooks.com

Illustrations by Viviana Moyana

The Homestead Kids Book Series www.thehomesteadkidsbooks.com

Illustrations by Viviana Moyana

The Homestead Kids Book Series　　　　　www.thehomesteadkidsbooks.com

Illustrations by Viviana Moyana

The Homestead Kids Book Series　　　　　　　www.thehomesteadkidsbooks.com

Illustrations by Viviana Moyana

The Homestead Kids Book Series   www.thehomesteadkidsbooks.com

Illustrations by Viviana Moyana

The Homestead Kids Book Series www.thehomesteadkidsbooks.com

Illustrations by Viviana Moyana

The Homestead Kids Book Series　　　　　　　www.thehomesteadkidsbooks.com

Illustrations by Viviana Moyana

The Homestead Kids Book Series www.thehomesteadkidsbooks.com

Illustrations by Viviana Moyana

The Homestead Kids Book Series   www.thehomesteadkidsbooks.com

Illustrations by Viviana Moyana

The Homestead Kids Book Series   www.thehomesteadkidsbooks.com

Illustrations by Viviana Moyana

The Homestead Kids Book Series   www.thehomesteadkidsbooks.com

Illustrations by Viviana Moyana

The Homestead Kids Book Series　　　www.thehomesteadkidsbooks.com

Illustrations by Viviana Moyana

The Homestead Kids Book Series www.thehomesteadkidsbooks.com

Illustrations by Viviana Moyana

The Homestead Kids Book Series   www.thehomesteadkidsbooks.com

Illustrations by Viviana Moyana

The Homestead Kids Book Series www.thehomesteadkidsbooks.com

Illustrations by Viviana Moyana

The Homestead Kids Book Series   www.thehomesteadkidsbooks.com

Illustrations by Viviana Moyana

The Homestead Kids Book Series   www.thehomesteadkidsbooks.com

Illustrations by Viviana Moyana

The Homestead Kids Book Series	www.thehomesteadkidsbooks.com

Illustrations by Viviana Moyana

Made in the USA
Middletown, DE
26 August 2024

59778567R00049